Orchard Books, an imprint of Scholastic Inc.
95 Madison Avenue, New York, NY 10016

Manufactured in the United States of America
Printed and bound by Phoenix Color Corp.
Book design by Zara Design

The text of this book is set in 16 point Esprit Medium.
The illustrations are acrylic.

2   4   6   8   10   9   7   5   3   1

Library of Congress Cataloging-in-Publication Data
Johnson, Paul Brett.
The goose who went off in a huff / Paul Brett Johnson.
p. cm.
Summary: Magnolia the goose longs to be a mother and finally gets her
wish in a most unusual way after a circus leaves town.
ISBN 0-531-30317-9 (tr. : alk. paper)
[1. Geese—Fiction. 2. Elephants—Fiction.
3. Animals—Infancy—Fiction.
4. Mother and child—Fiction.] I. Title.
PZ7.J6354 Go 2001 [E]—dc21 00-39964

THE Goose Who Went Off IN A Huff

by
Paul Brett Johnson

Orchard Books ★ New York
An Imprint of Scholastic Inc.

When Magnolia took George's rubber ducky for a walk, Miss Rosemary didn't suspect a thing. "Magnolia, you've upset George. Please ask before you play with someone else's toys."

When Magnolia tried to hatch Easter eggs,
Miss Rosemary still didn't catch on. "Magnolia!
Those eggs are for the Easter Social," she scolded.

But when Magnolia tried to give swimming lessons to Dotty Sue's baby chicks, Miss Rosemary finally started to wonder. "Magnolia, you silly goose! What's gotten into you? It's a known fact that chickens don't swim. You nearly drowned the poor darlings."

Magnolia watched longingly as Dotty Sue fussed over her dripping brood. Suddenly it all became clear. "I should have guessed," said Miss Rosemary. "Magnolia wants to be a mama. Well, quit your fretting, dear. That sort of thing happens in its own good time. Now you leave Dotty Sue's babies be. Everyone knows that chicks go with chickens and goslings go with geese."

Miss Rosemary hoped that would be the end of that. But Magnolia seemed to be in no mood for good advice. With a haughty honk, she waddled off. "There's no need to go pout," Miss Rosemary called after her.

The rest of that day Magnolia was nowhere to be seen. Miss Rosemary wasn't worried though. "I suppose Magnolia is a little embarrassed. Perhaps she just needs some time alone."

But when her goose did not show up for supper, Miss Rosemary grew concerned. It wasn't like Magnolia to miss a meal. "Maybe I was a bit too stern with the poor dear," she fretted.

Before going to bed, Miss Rosemary checked the barn. "Has anyone seen Magnolia?" No one had.

That night Miss Rosemary tossed and turned. She had a dreadful dream about a troupe of circus acrobats.

Horrified, Miss Rosemary sprang up in bed. "Merciful Moses!" she cried. "Magnolia has run away from home!"

The next morning Miss Rosemary organized a search party. They went to the circus grounds and peeked in every tent. There were bears and elephants and monkeys and lions, but there wasn't a goose anywhere.

On the way home, they walked along the railroad tracks. "Magnolia? Magnoooo-lia!"

They stopped off at the swimming hole. But the missing goose was nowhere to be seen.

Finally Miss Rosemary took one last look in the shed. She was about to give up hope when a couple of suspicious-looking tail feathers caught her eye.

Miss Rosemary tiptoed back outside and whispered to Gertrude and George, "Magnolia hasn't run away at all. She's only pretending. I think her feelings are hurt."

Miss Rosemary eased up beside the shed window. "I do hope Magnolia hasn't run away from home," she said loudly. "We all really miss her. It just won't be the same around here." Miss Rosemary waited.

"If only Magnolia were here I would bake a fat, scrumptious blueberry pie. It's a known fact that blueberry is Magnolia's favorite. She could have the biggest piece!"

There was still no movement inside the shed.

Quite obviously, the situation called for more drastic
measures. Miss Rosemary, George, and Gertrude went back
to the house to think.

A while later Miss Rosemary returned to the shed.
"Land o' Goshen!" she exclaimed. "Just look at those two
little goslings. Poor sweet things, no sign of their mama.
They must be orphans. Who's going to look after them?"

"*Monk, monk,*" said Gertrude.
"*Hoink, hoink,*" said George.
Magnolia did not even rustle a feather.
Miss Rosemary sighed. What in the world
was she going to do about her goose?

That afternoon Miss Rosemary heard a rumble down by the railroad tracks and a shrill cry that sounded a bit like a trumpet. *"RrrrUUUUUUUUUUUUmph!"*

"What in thunderation was that?" she wondered.

Miss Rosemary went to investigate.

It was only the circus train leaving town.
Miss Rosemary waved and watched until the
caboose finally rolled by.

As she turned to leave, Miss Rosemary heard the curious wail again. *"RrrrUUUUUUUUUUUUUmph!"*

Something was thrashing in the bushes beside the track.

"Wait! Wait!" she yelled after the train. "I think you've left someone behind!" But it was too late. The train had already disappeared.

Suddenly a very long nose snaked out of the bushes . . .

followed by a pair of small, frightened eyes . . .

surrounded by two huge floppy ears.

"Oh my goodness. Isn't this a fine mess!" Miss Rosemary scratched her head in puzzlement. "Chicks go with chickens and goslings go with geese—that's a known fact. But what in the world do little lost elephants go with?"

Magnolia had the answer to that.